Popcorn vs Nacho

by Nation Chapman

DEDICATION

To my mom and dad. Love you.

"Come on, David. We don't want to miss the movie," says David's mom. David quickly grabs his popcorn and nachos, and rushes into the dark theater with his parents.

David hurries to the top of the stairs
and picks the seat between
his mom and dad.

As David fumbles to unfold
his seat, a piece of popcorn
falls into the nacho bowl.

While David is watching the movie,
the little popcorn that fell into the bowl
is suddenly surrounded by the nachos!

The nachos were shocked to see
the little popcorn there.

The nachos were shoved out of the way
as a Giant nacho marched forward.

The Giant nacho wasn't nice to anyone.
He shouted at the little popcorn...

The little popcorn was afraid
and didn't know what to do.

All of a sudden, a hand-shaped shadow
appeared over the bowl! David
was ready for a snack.

The little popcorn and nachos began screaming and running away.

The Giant nacho tried to escape,
but he was too slow.

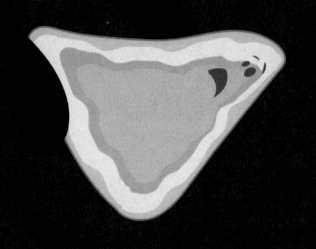

David was unaware of the
fight and picked up the
delicious, Giant nacho.

Then, there was
a loud...

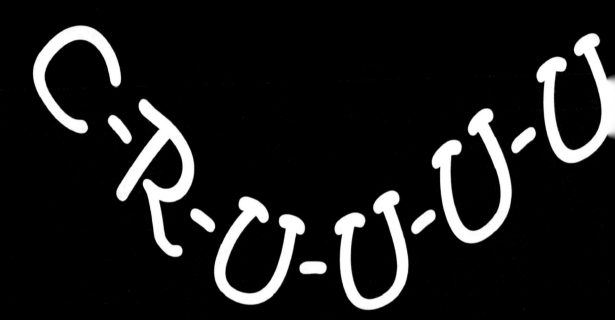

C-R-U-U-U-U

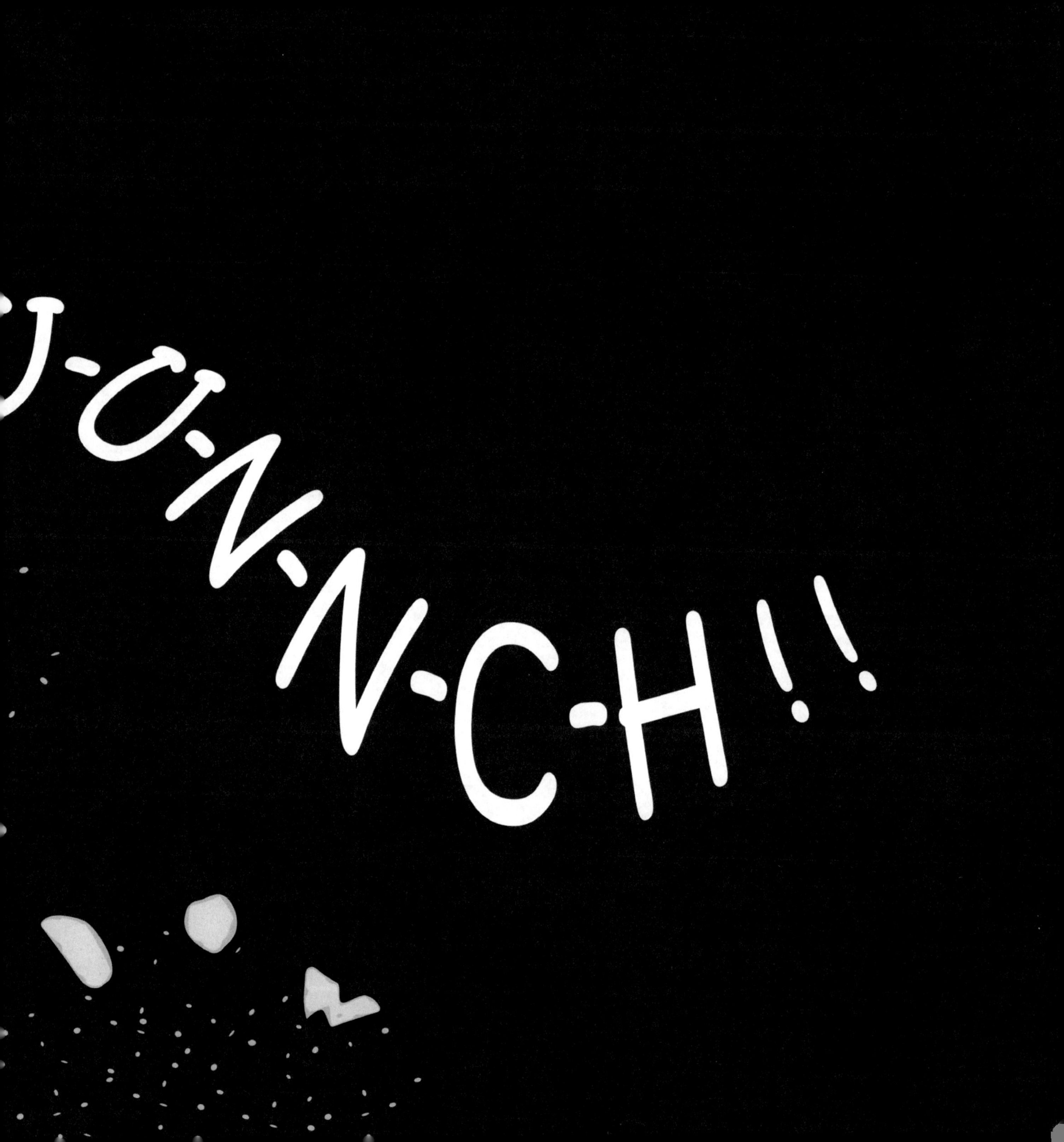
-U-N-N-C-H!!

The little popcorn was saved!
The other nachos were also relieved
because the Giant nacho could
not bully them anymore.

So the little popcorn and the nachos
ALL cheered with joy!

THE END

I thank you for reading my book because my book is very awesome! One day I hope you write your own book just like me. All you have to do is ask your mom or dad.

Made in the USA
Middletown, DE
25 March 2017